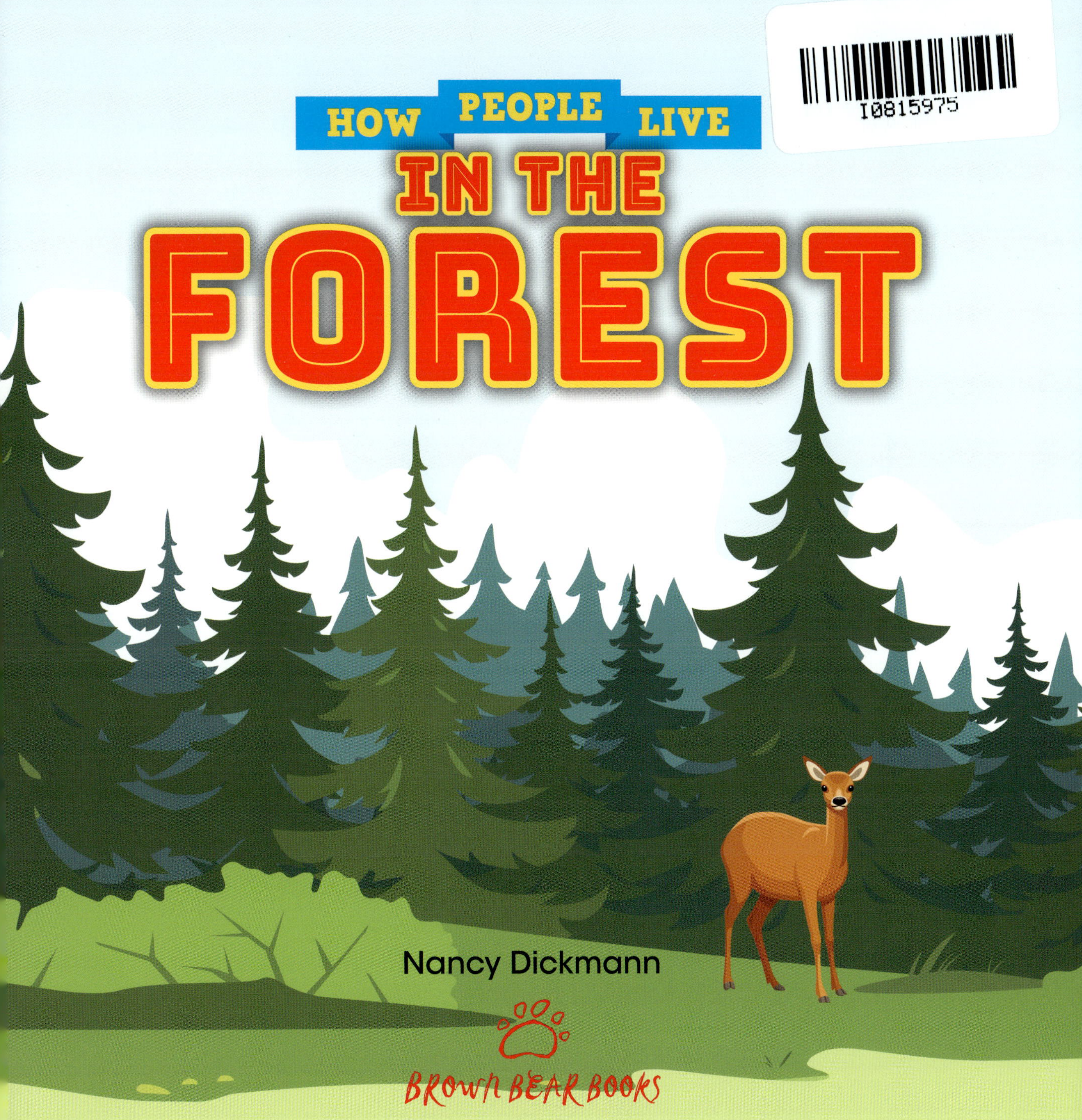

HOW PEOPLE LIVE

IN THE FOREST

Nancy Dickmann

BROWN BEAR BOOKS

Published by Brown Bear Books Ltd
4877 N. Circulo Bujia, Tucson, AZ 85718, USA
and
Studio G14, Regent Studios, 1 Thane Villas, London N7 7PH, UK

Text: Nancy Dickmann
Design Manager: Keith Davis
Children's Publisher: Anne O'Daly

Library of Congress Cataloging-in-Publication Data
Names: Dickmann, Nancy, author.
Title: In the forest / Nancy Dickmann. Other titles: How people live in forests
Description: Tuscon, AZ : Brown Bear Books, [2025] | Series: Fast track: how people live | Includes bibliographical references and index. | Audience: Ages 5-7. | Audience: Grades K-1. | Summary: "How people live in forests all around the world"– Provided by publisher.
Identifiers: LCCN 2023052209 (print) | LCCN 2023052210 (ebook) | ISBN 9781781219720 (library binding) | ISBN 9781781219782 (paperback) | ISBN 9781781219843 (ebook)
Subjects: LCSH: Communities–Juvenile literature. | Sociology, Rural–Juvenile literature. | Forests and forestry–Juvenile literature. | Forestry and community–Juvenile literature.
Classification: LCC HT421 .D53 2025 (print) | LCC HT421 (ebook) | DDC 307.72–dc23/eng/20231221
LC record available at https://lccn.loc.gov/2023052209
LC ebook record available at https://lccn.loc.gov/2023052210

The photographs in this book are used by permission and through the courtesy of:
Cover: Shutterstock: Gulseren Onder. Interior: iStock: Alonzo Design 6-7bk, 14-15bk, Alex Coolok 8-9bk, 16-17bk, Halyna Lakatosh 1, 2-3, 20-21k, 22-23bk, 24, LL28 20t; Shutterstock: ActiveLines 4-5bk, 10-11bk, 12-13bk, 18-19bk , ASB63 13, Tetyana Dotsenko 15, freedomnaruk 10, Eizaveta Galitckaia 18, Elmar Gubisch 14, Elena Istomina 24b, Donna Kasubeck 11, Kertu 17, 21t, maruco 19, Joao Mello 20b, milosk50 5, My Ticklefeet 16, netacabo 21b, Paulo Jr 12, Piu-Piu 6, Andrej Puchta 23, Cally Robin 4, Paul Tessier 9, Sergey Uryadnikov 8, 21cr, Maarten Zeehandelaar 7.
t-top, b-bottom, l-left, r-right, c-center, bk-background
All other artwork and photography © Brown Bear Books.

Words in **bold** appear in the Words to Know on page 23.

Manufactured in the United States of America
CPSIA compliance information: Batch#AG/5659

Contents

Among the Trees

Tall trees reach toward the sky.
Smaller plants hug the ground.
The shaded ground is covered in leaves.
This is a forest. Forests are beautiful places.

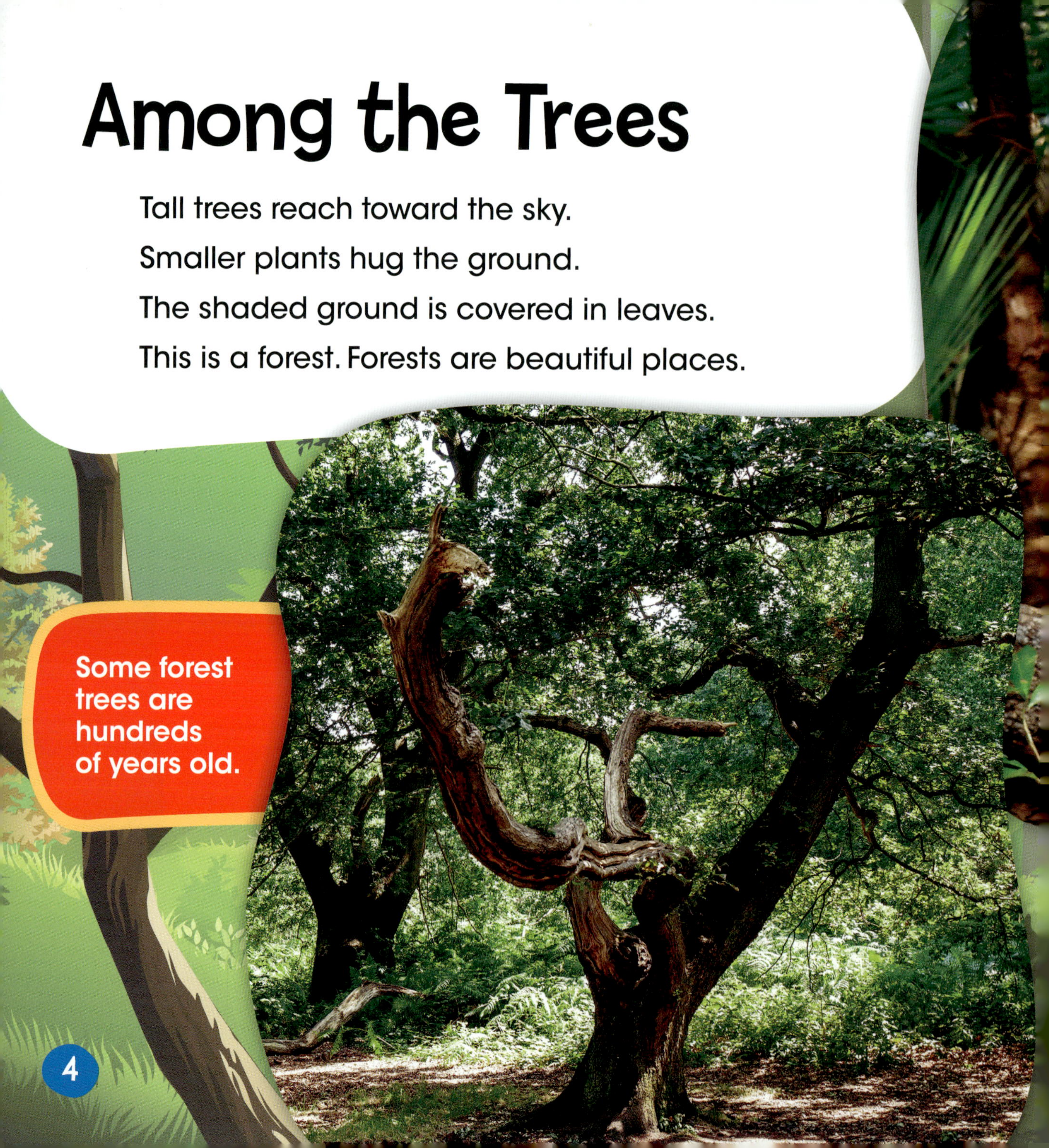

Some forest trees are hundreds of years old.

There are forests all over the world. They are home to many different animals. Some live on the ground. Others live in the trees. People live in forests, too.

Weather and Climate

A **temperate** forest is warm in summer.
It is cold in winter. Its trees lose their leaves in fall.
In the spring, the leaves grow again.
Other forests are in colder places.

In cold forests, trees have needles instead of leaves.

Some forests get a lot of rain.

They are called **rain forests**.

Many rain forests are near the **Equator**.

They are hot and steamy.

WOW!

The Amazon is the world's largest rain forest. It's almost eight times as big as Texas!

Forest Homes

Many forest homes are made of wood.
There is plenty of wood in a forest.
People also use other **natural materials**.
Sometimes roofs are made of leaves or grass.

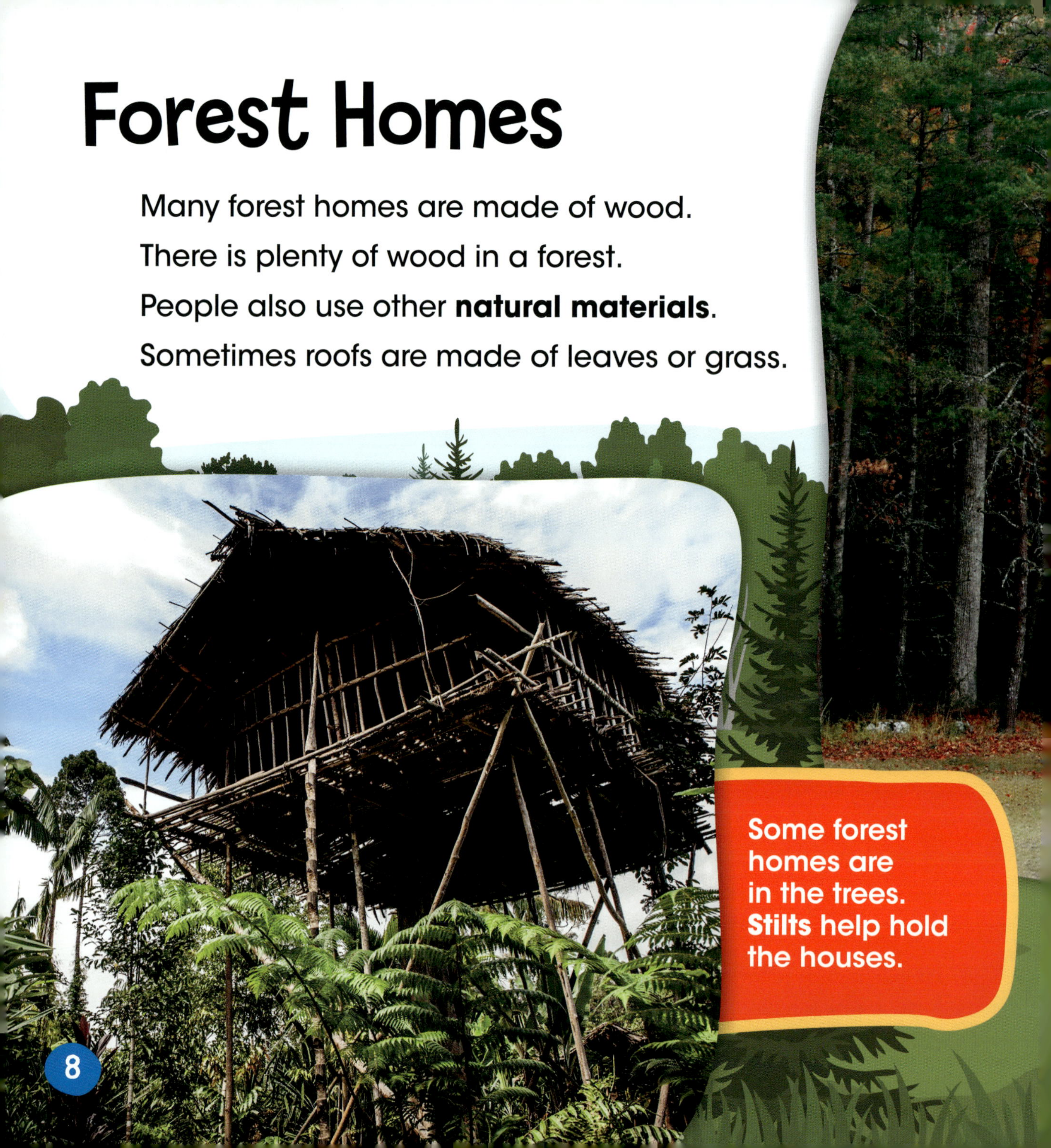

Some forest homes are in the trees. **Stilts** help hold the houses.

Forests cover much of the eastern United States. People built log cabins. Long logs make the walls. Gaps were filled with mud. Many people still build wooden homes there.

Food and Drink

Plants grow well in rain forests. Bananas and avocados come from rain forests. So do coffee, vanilla, and many nuts. But too much farming can harm forests.

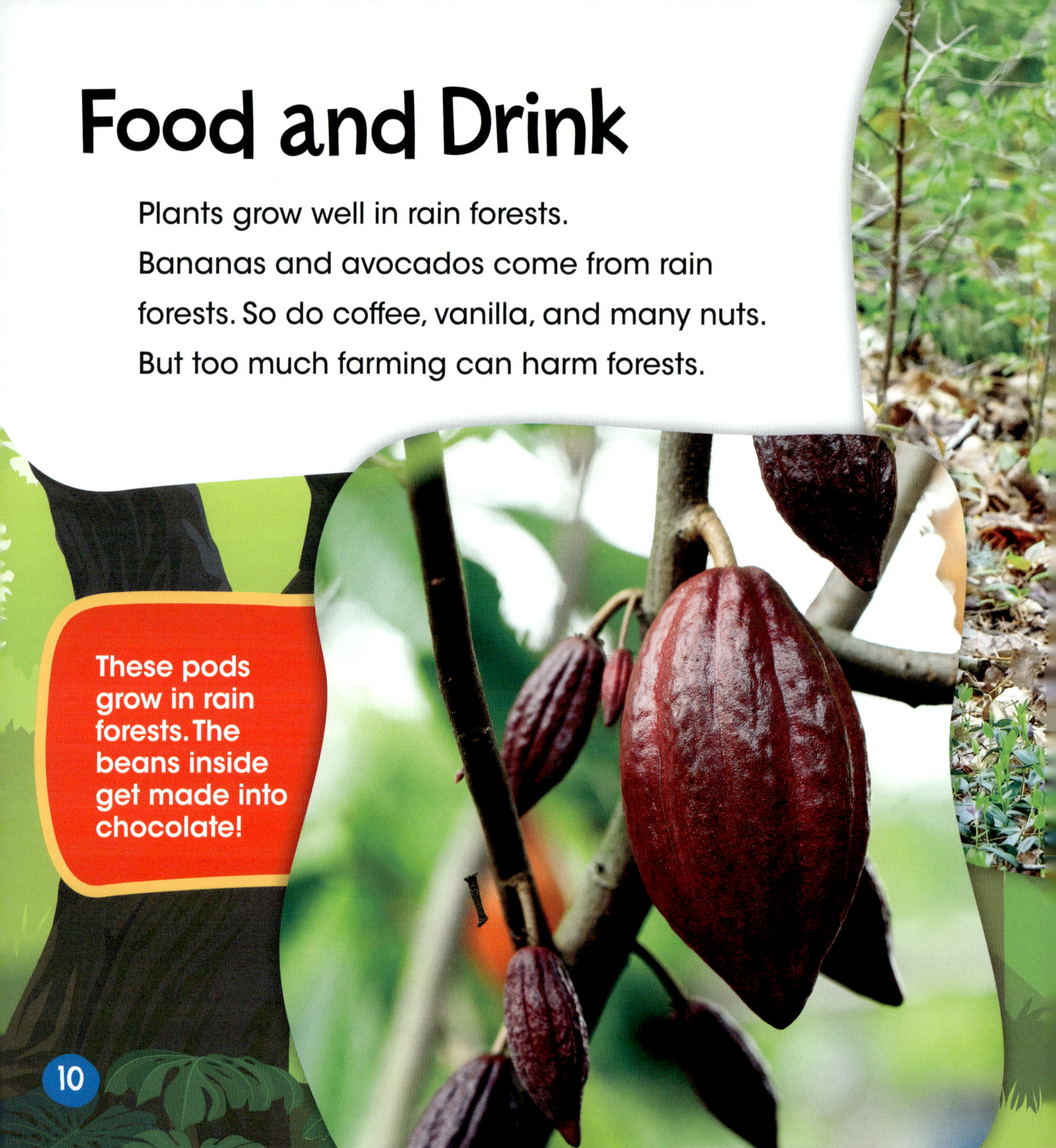

These pods grow in rain forests. The beans inside get made into chocolate!

Some people hunt forest animals.
In temperate forests, they hunt wild turkeys.
In cold forests, some people **herd** reindeer.
They drink their milk.

Clothes

Many rain forests are hot and damp.
People choose clothes to stay cool.
They might wear shorts and t-shirts.
Some rain forest people wear very little.

Some people make clothes from natural materials. They use plants and feathers.

Other forests are cold and windy.
People made clothes from skins and furs.
Now many wear coats with feathers inside.
The feathers keep them warm.

Jobs

Some people work as **loggers**. They cut down trees. The wood is used for furniture and paper. People plant new trees to replace them. They work to keep the forest healthy.

Being a logger is hard work. It can be dangerous.

WOW!

Some rangers watch for smoke from a high tower. If they spot a fire quickly, it will be easier to put out.

Today, many forests are under threat. Too many trees are cut down. Fires destroy others. **Rangers** work to protect forests. They check that plants are healthy. They keep animals safe.

Getting Around

Trees grow close together in many forests. It's hard to build roads. People travel along the forest's rivers. Boats and canoes are common in the Amazon rain forest.

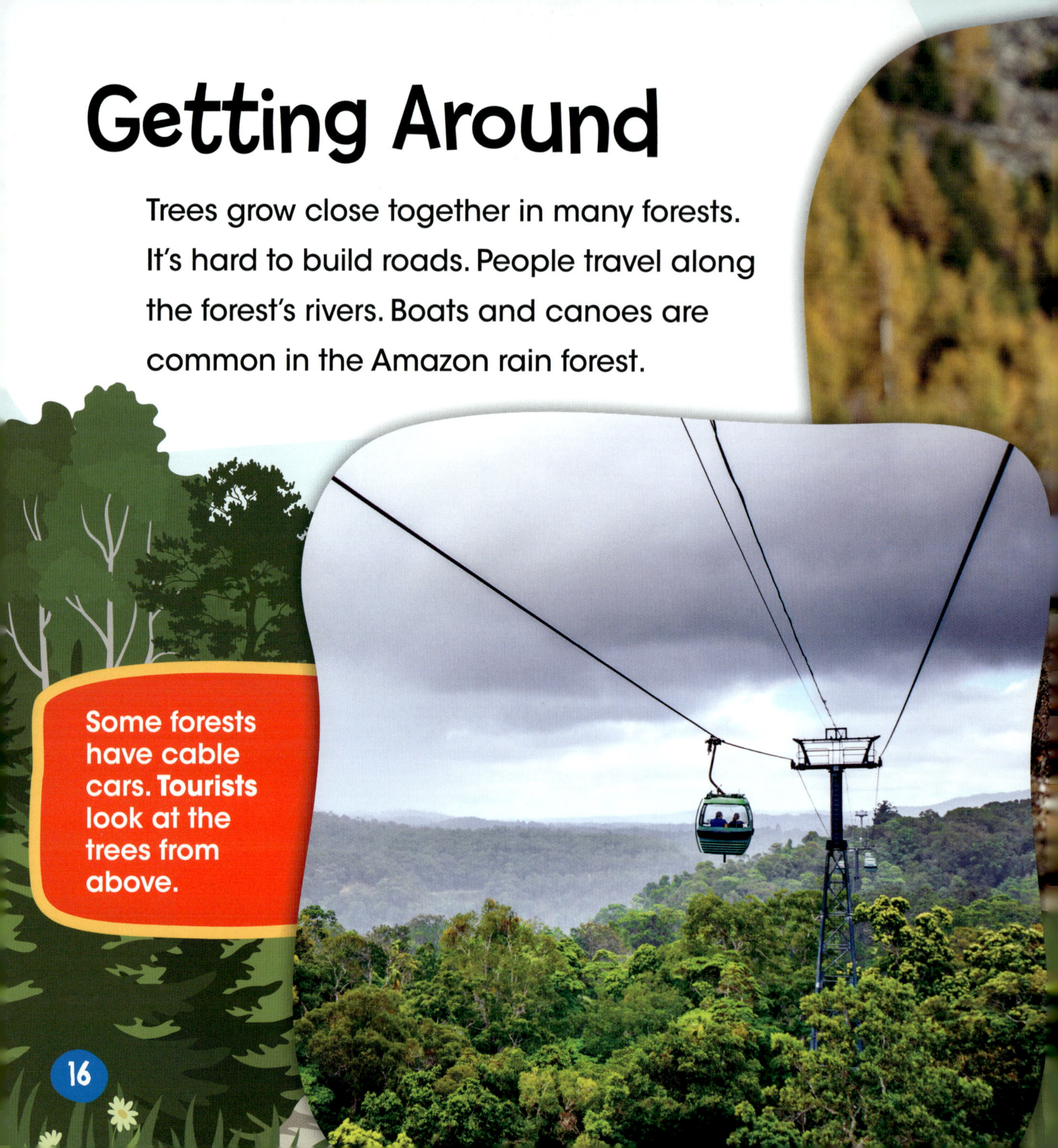

Some forests have cable cars. **Tourists** look at the trees from above.

Many forest people get around by walking. They use the sun to find their way. Other people ride horses. Some people in cold forests ride reindeer!

Games and Sports

Forests are great places to hike.
People often camp in forests.
Some forests have zip lines.
People zoom above the trees.

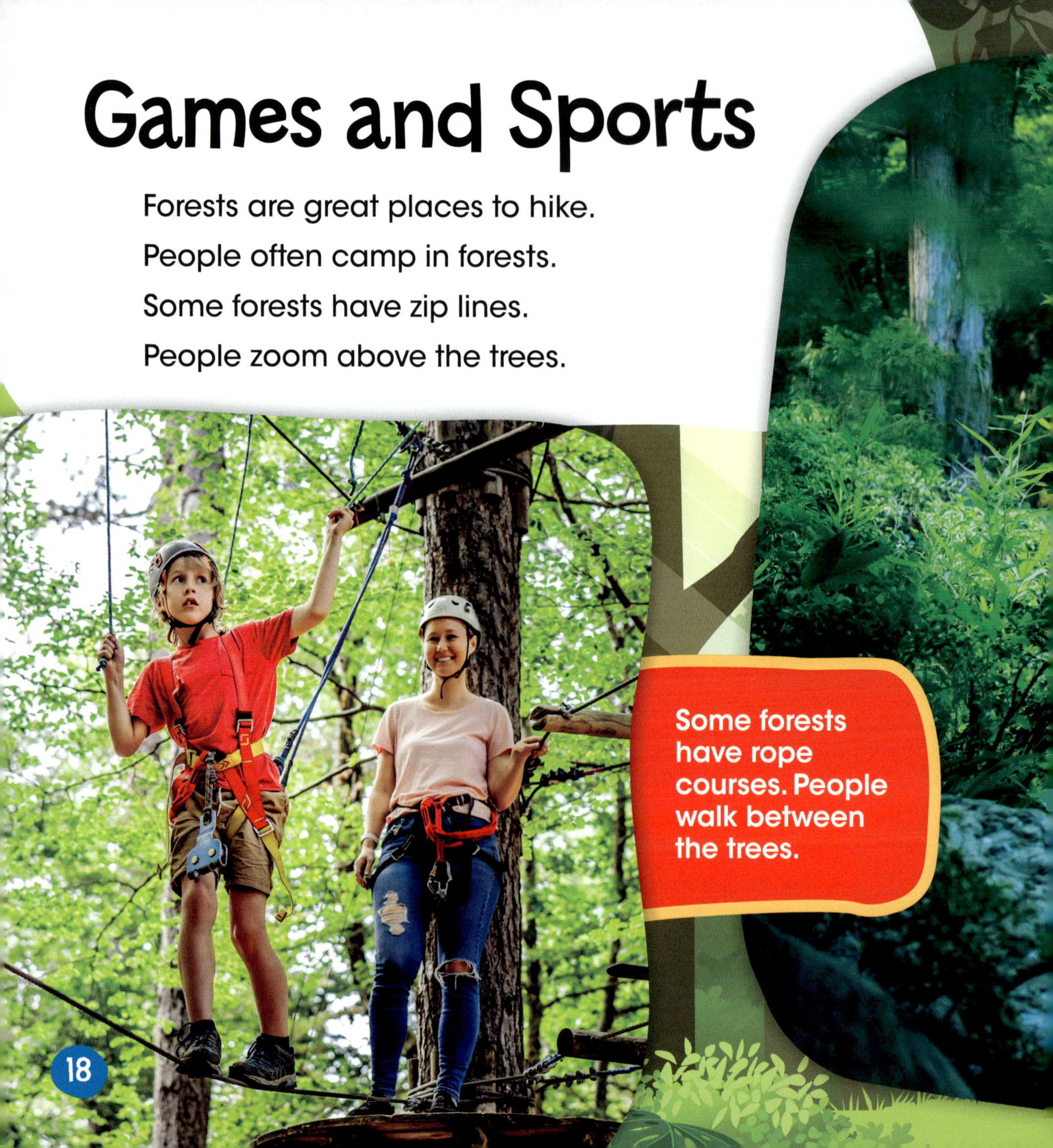

Some forests have rope courses. People walk between the trees.

Forest bathing started in Japan.
People relax among the trees.
They breathe deeply. They look at nature.
It helps them feel calm.

Where in the World?

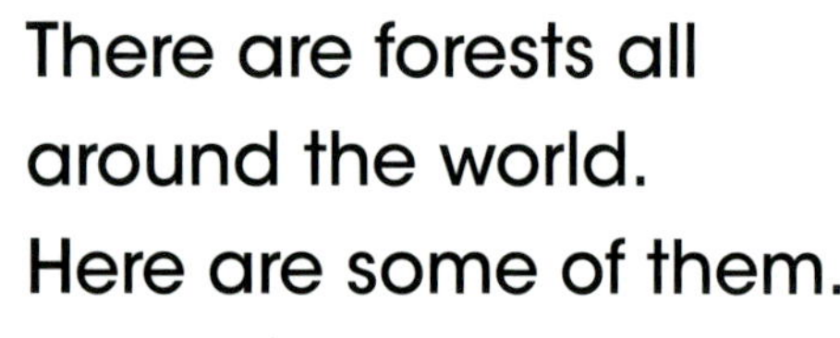

There are forests all around the world. Here are some of them.

People love to visit giant sequoia forests in California.

Many people in the Amazon wear traditional clothes.

Groups of herders live in the cold forests of Russia and Mongolia.

Many different groups live in the rain forests of Indonesia.

People in the Congo share the rain forest with gorillas and other animals.

Activities

Look on a map to find the forest that is closest to where you live. What kind of forest is it? How far away is it? How would you get there?

Look around your home. How many different things can you that are made from trees. Don't forget that paper comes from wood!

Rain forests are home to many animals. Choose one and research it. How does it live? Is its habitat under threat?

Find Out More

Websites

dkfindout.com/us/animals-and-nature/habitats-and-ecosystems/amazon-rain-forest/

kids.britannica.com/kids/article/forest/390614

kids.nationalgeographic.com/nature/habitats/article/temperate-forest

Books

Forest Biomes Around the World Christine Elizabeth Eboch, Capstone Press 2020

Rain Forest Biomes Cecilia Pinto McCarthy, Abdo Publishing 2024

Living in the Rain Forest Alicia Z. Klepeis, Rosen Publishing 2021

Words to Know

Equator an imaginary line around the middle of the Earth, where the weather is usually warm all year

herd to gather and take care of a group of animals, moving them from place to place

logger a person whose job is cutting down trees so that their wood can be used

natural material a material that comes from a living thing, such as grass, wood, or feathers

rain forest a dense forest that gets a lot of rain; rain forests can be hot or cool

ranger a person whose job is to patrol and protect a natural area such as a forest

temperate having a climate that is warm in summer and cool in winter

stilts long poles that help to support a house or other structure that is raised off the ground

tourist a person who travels to a place on vacation to see the sights

Index